THE PUP

TRIXIE

THE PUPPY PLACE

Don't miss any of the
other stories by Ellen Miles!

THE PUPPY PLACE

TRIXIE

ELLEN MILES

SCHOLASTIC INC.

Copyright © 2024 by Ellen Miles
Cover art by Tim O'Brien
Original cover design by Steve Scott

ISBN 978-1-339-01229-2

10 9 8 7 6 5 4 3 2 1   24 25 26 27 28

Printed in the U.S.A.   40

First printing 2024

CHAPTER ONE

Lizzie Peterson stepped into her house after school one sunny, crisp October day.

"Nooooooo!" came a wail from upstairs.

"Oh, man," Lizzie said. She covered her ears. "Whoa." Nobody could wail as loudly as her youngest brother, the Bean. When he got really wound up, you could hear him from a block away. Fortunately for the Peterson family and for their neighbors, the Bean was almost always in a good mood. But when he was feeling cranky, watch out!

The trouble was, the Bean seemed to be feeling cranky a lot lately. Not that it was totally his fault. He kept coming home from day care with runny-nose colds, or itchy rashes, or an upset tummy. Every week it was something different. He was hardly ever sick enough to stay in bed, but he was too sick to go to day care. Lizzie hated being sick, so she could understand why it made the Bean cranky.

Unfortunately, the situation also made the whole family cranky. Dad was cranky because he almost always caught the cold, or rash, or tummy problem. Mom was cranky because she was working on a big article for the newspaper and her deadline was getting closer. When the Bean was home from day care, it was almost impossible for her to get much done besides taking care of him.

Charles, Lizzie's other brother, was cranky because he just couldn't take it when the Bean cried. "Why does he have to be so noisy?" Charles would ask Lizzie. "I wasn't that noisy when I was his age, was I?"

"Dream on," Lizzie told him, rolling her eyes. "You were even worse."

Lizzie was cranky because she couldn't decide what she wanted to dress as for Halloween. Plus, Mom kept asking her to help out with the Bean. For some reason, Lizzie was the one who could always calm him down. She loved her brother, she really did—but she didn't always love getting stuck with cheering him up.

If the Bean were a puppy, that would be different. Lizzie could put up with anything if it meant she got to spend time with a puppy. Barking puppies, nipping puppies, peeing puppies—she'd seen it all, since the Petersons were a foster family who specialized in caring for puppies who needed homes.

Of course, Lizzie's puppy, Buddy, was not a barker, or a nipper, or a pee-er—at least most of the time. Buddy was the cutest puppy ever. Buddy

3

was the one puppy that the Petersons hadn't been able to give up when the time came to find him a forever family. Lizzie guessed that at this moment Buddy was probably out in the fenced backyard, hiding under the rosebushes so he wouldn't have to hear the Bean's tantrum.

Lizzie was about to go find Buddy when Mom appeared in the kitchen with the Bean riding on her hip. He was basically yelling into her ear at the top of his lungs. "Don't waaaaaannnnn-naaaaa!" he bawled.

Mom looked frazzled. Her hair stuck up in weird places, her sweater had gross-looking stains on it, and her socks were mismatched. She gave Lizzie a crooked smile and raised one eyebrow. "Fun day," she said. "He never even went down for his nap."

"I'll take him," Lizzie said before her mother

could even ask. She could see that Mom really needed her help. Plus, it was hard to see her little brother so upset. She knew exactly how to cheer him up.

"I'll bring him along on my route," Lizzie said.

"Oh, that'd be great," Mom said. "Thank you, Lizzie. I mean it."

Lizzie grabbed her backpack from the row of hooks by the kitchen door and took an apple from the bowl on the counter. Then she held her arms out to the Bean. "Come on, let's go see some puppies!"

The Bean stopped wailing. He squirmed out of Mom's arms and ran to Lizzie. "Uppies?" He pulled on Lizzie's hand. "Yet's go!"

Lizzie and some friends had a dog-walking business, and every day after school Lizzie headed out to exercise the dogs on her route. It was more like play than work, Lizzie always thought. Who wouldn't want to be around dogs all the time? Sometimes she couldn't believe that she actually got paid to hang out with so many fun pals. AAA Dynamic Dog Walkers (that was the name of the business) had been one of her best ideas ever.

"Lizzie!" The Bean pulled on her arm again. "C'mon!"

The Bean loved to join Lizzie on her dog-walking route. The only problem was that he walked so slowly. Sometimes Lizzie felt like she was about to be yanked in half when there was a dog pulling her one way and the Bean pulling her the other.

"Hold on," said Lizzie. "I just need my sweat-shirt." She reached into her backpack and pulled out her oldest, most treasured piece of clothing. She loved it because it was comfortable and soft and warm. Best of all, it was covered with funny drawings of all the dog breeds.

"Really?" Mom asked, crossing her arms and raising an eyebrow.

Lizzie smiled. Mom had tried to throw the sweatshirt away so many times, but Lizzie always rescued it. So what if the cuffs were ragged and there were stains down the front? Once it had been white, and now it was, well, sort of grayish. And one of the elbows was gone. But it was Lizzie's dog-walking uniform, her lucky charm. Lizzie pulled it on. As always, it felt cozy and comforting and so familiar. She twirled around as if she were modeling the shirt.

Mom laughed. "Okay, fine. Thanks for taking the Bean, Lizzie," Mom said. "And don't forget—never—"

"Never let go of his hand," Lizzie said. "I know."

She was proud that Mom had been trusting her to take care of her brother. "I promise."

"What about your doggie?" Lizzie asked the Bean as they got ready to go. She reached into her backpack and pulled out a blue leash.

The Bean jumped up and down in excitement, then took the leash. Moments later, he and Lizzie headed down the street. The Bean trailed the leash—and his imaginary dog—behind him. He gripped Lizzie's hand as he trotted along beside her, all his crankiness forgotten. "Uppy!" he said.

"Yes, we're going to see some puppies," Lizzie agreed, smiling down at him.

"Uppy!" the Bean said, louder. He pointed down the street.

Lizzie looked, but she didn't see anything. "Okay," she said, shrugging her shoulders.

"Over there!" the Bean yelled, pointing again.

This time, Lizzie saw it. A blur of white and brown, dashing across the street. "Hey!" she said. "Is that a—puppy?"

CHAPTER TWO

Lizzie's heart began to pound. What was a puppy doing out here by herself? She pulled the Bean's hand. "Come on!" she said. "We have to find her."

"Wait!" the Bean said. "My dog is sniffing." He looked back at the empty end of his leash.

Lizzie had taught her brother that it was good to let dogs sniff as much as they wanted. "That's how they learn about the world," she'd explained. "It's like when grown-ups read the newspaper or listen to the radio. Dogs get information from sniffing things, like who has been there before. We can be patient and wait for them."

Now, Lizzie wished she'd never given him

that idea. "Argh!" she said. "Not now, Beany. We have to help that other puppy." The *real* one, she wanted to add, but she didn't. She just held his hand tighter and walked faster.

The Bean dawdled, looking back at his pretend friend.

"There!" Lizzie said. "There she is again!" The puppy ran through the backyard of the house they were passing, leaping over bushes and darting under a picnic table. This time, Lizzie got a good look at her. Short white fur with brown spots, a whippy little tail, and small ears, one perked (brown) and the other floppy (white). *Jack Russell mix,* Lizzie thought automatically. *Mixed with . . . Chihuahua, maybe?* Lizzie couldn't help herself. She had memorized her "Dog Breeds of the World" poster, and whenever she saw a dog— or even just had a glimpse of a dog—she did her best to identify it.

The Bean jumped up and down, yelling, as the puppy dashed through the next backyard and disappeared under a fence.

"Careful." Lizzie put a finger to her lips. "We don't want to scare the puppy," she said softly. She knew that when she spoke softly and calmly, the Bean usually calmed down, too.

The Bean stopped jumping. He put a finger to his own lips, raised his eyebrows high, and nodded his head quickly up and down.

Lizzie scanned the area. Where had that pesky puppy gone? And how was she going to catch her? It wasn't going to be easy with the Bean along. Then she straightened up. What was that? She thought she saw a little nose poking out from behind the small yellow house on the corner. "Oh! Over there!" she shouted, pointing. "Is that her?"

"Shhh! Don't scare uppy!" the Bean whispered loudly. He glared at Lizzie, his hands on his hips.

As upset as she was about the puppy, Lizzie had to laugh. "You're right!" she whispered back as she pulled him along in the direction of the yellow house. "We have to go slow and be gentle, like we always do with new puppies."

After being around so many foster puppies, the Bean understood how to behave around dogs he didn't know. He knew to keep his voice down, to move slowly, and not to run in for a hug; instead he kept quiet and still as he let a new dog check him out by sniffing his hand.

The Bean nodded as he trotted along, trying to keep up with Lizzie. "Dentle," he said, panting a little.

"Right, gentle," said Lizzie as they turned the corner by the yellow house. No puppy! Lizzie stopped and scanned again, sweeping her gaze from side to side. The little scamp! How far could she have gotten?

"There!" said the Bean, pointing behind Lizzie.

Lizzie whirled around just in time to see the puppy dash away, back toward where they'd first spotted her. "Argh!" she cried. "How did she even get over that way?" Lizzie was sure she'd been watching for her the whole time. This girl was fast—and tricky!

"You know, I don't think we're going to catch that puppy by ourselves," Lizzie said to the Bean. She knew she should probably find an adult to help, but she was in a rush. "We've got to go find Maria and the others."

The Bean grinned. "Ria, Ria, Ria!" He loved Lizzie's best friend, Maria Santiago.

Lizzie knew where Maria would be, three blocks away on her own dog-walking route. Too bad Lizzie's parents refused to let her have a phone until she was thirteen. She could have just texted

Maria. But there was no time to waste; they had to run. "Let's go!"

She and the Bean took off as fast as they could, Lizzie holding tightly to her little brother's hand. His leash trailed behind him, his pretend dog forgotten in the excitement of the moment.

"Maria!" Lizzie called when she spotted her friend at the other end of the street. She waved at Maria. "Hey! We need you!"

Maria sprinted toward them. She was with Pogo and Pixie, twin Poodles who were always ready for a run.

Panting, Lizzie explained about the puppy. "We've got to catch her," she finished. "Can you text Brianna and Daphne?" Maria's parents had given her a phone—"only for emergencies!"—a few months ago. "Tell them to meet us at the corner of Summer and Vine streets." Brianna and Daphne were the other partners in AAA Dynamic Dog Walkers.

"Good idea." Maria nodded and pulled out her phone, texting with both thumbs like a teenager. "I'll run Pogo and Pixie home and meet you over there as soon as I can."

"Great," said Lizzie. "I'll figure out a plan by the time you all get there." She paused, wondering if she should tell Maria to call Mom, too. Lizzie knew she was supposed to find an adult to help if she spotted a stray dog. But Mom was so busy and she really needed some time to get her article done. Plus, Lizzie had seen this puppy; she wasn't the ferocious type. Four experienced dog walkers should be able to handle one very small dog.

At least, she hoped they could. Lizzie thought about it as she and the Bean trotted back toward the yellow house. How to catch a puppy? She'd had a little practice with other stray dogs, but she had to slow down her brain and remember all the steps. "Don't scare her," she mumbled to herself. "Have good treats." She felt in her pocket for the biscuits she always carried, and remembered the string cheese she'd grabbed from the fridge. "Perfect. Dogs could never resist cheese."

What else? *Don't approach too fast,* she thought. *In fact, pretending to run away or looking at something very, very interesting on the ground can bring a curious dog running toward you. And never—*

"Uppy!" the Bean yelled.

CHAPTER THREE

The Bean was right again. There was the puppy, and for once she was not racing along. Lizzie finally got a really good look at her, and she was so cute! She was sniffing at the bottom of a big maple tree; her nose was thrust deep down into a pile of golden-yellow leaves. She snuffled away, not noticing as Lizzie and the Bean came toward her, very quietly and slowly. The Bean was on tippy-toes, a finger over his lips. "Shhh," he whispered. "Don't scare her!"

Lizzie gave his hand a squeeze. "We won't," she whispered back. "We'll just see if we can get a tiny bit closer." She was tiptoeing, too.

Suddenly, the dog's head flew up, both ears perked. She'd heard them! She swiveled her head this way and that until she spotted Lizzie and the Bean. Then, in a blur of white and brown, she was gone.

"Argh!" cried Lizzie for the third time that day. This was so frustrating.

"I sorry! I was quiet," the Bean said. His eyes brimmed with tears and Lizzie could see that he was about to start wailing.

"It's okay, it's okay," she said, kneeling down to give him a hug. "Soon the others will be here and we'll have another chance to catch the puppy."

When she stood up, she saw Maria, Daphne, and Brianna running toward them. And—was that the Santiagos's car? Lizzie watched as Mr. Santiago parked the car. She raised an eyebrow at Maria, who had just arrived, breathing hard, at her side.

"Yup, I called my parents," Maria said. "You know

we're supposed to. And I thought Simba could help."

"Simba!" yelled the Bean.

Lizzie turned to see Simba, a huge, gentle golden lab, climb out of the car. He was wearing a special red jacket and a harness with a handle that Mrs. Santiago was holding. Mrs. Santiago was blind, and Simba was her guide dog. He was the smartest, best-behaved dog Lizzie knew.

"Good idea," Lizzie said. Maria looked relieved.

"So, what's the plan?" Daphne asked. She and Brianna had caught up, and now everyone stood on the sidewalk in a circle, looking expectantly at Lizzie.

Lizzie gulped. She didn't really have a plan. But— now that Simba was here, maybe she did! "I think we should walk Simba up and down the street here. If the puppy sees another dog, especially one as friendly as Simba, maybe she'll be tempted to check him out. But—not all of us should do that," she went on as the plan took shape in her head. "Just me and Maria's mom. Everyone else should fan out in the neighborhood and let us know if you spot her."

They all nodded. They seemed to like the plan.

"Me, too?" asked the Bean.

"Of course, you, too," Lizzie said, and smiled down at him. "You're sticking with me." She turned to her friends. "Do the rest of you have spare leashes with you?" She knew that like her, they usually carried backpacks with all the equipment they might need for dog walking. They all nodded again.

"And we brought this." Maria's dad opened the trunk of his car and lifted out a dog crate.

"Wow, great thinking! Let's set it up and put some special treats inside it," Lizzie said. "I bet this puppy is hungry if she's been on the run for a while, and if she smells food, she might just wander into that crate."

"I'll keep an eye out and shut the door if she does go in," said Mr. Santiago. "Don't worry, we'll catch her."

Just then, the Bean tugged at Lizzie's hand. "Uppy," he whispered. "Uppy!"

Lizzie turned to see the white-and-brown puppy peering at the group from behind a flaming red bush. Her head was cocked as if she was trying to understand what was going on.

What are all these people so excited about? It must be something interesting. And that dog looks really friendly.

The puppy wagged her little tail and took a few steps forward.

"Brianna, Daphne," Lizzie whispered. "Circle around and get in back of her."

They nodded. Slowly, slowly, they moved so

that they were cutting off the puppy's options for escape. Mr. Santiago shifted as well. Then they all started to walk toward one another, again very slowly. The puppy ignored them; she was too busy staring at Simba. She pushed her paws out front and her butt in the air. Her little tail wagged fast.

Want to play? It's been a while since I've had some good playtime.

Simba looked up at Maria's mom.

"Simba wants to know if he can play with the puppy," Maria whispered to her mother.

"Go on, have fun," said Mrs. Santiago, letting go of Simba's harness.

He knew what that meant! Soon he and the puppy were circling each other, tails wagging as they sniffed and sniffed.

Simba seemed to know exactly what to do. As

he and the puppy checked each other out, the big dog moved closer and closer to the dog crate. Mr. Santiago crept closer and closer, too. Finally, Maria's dad was able to reach out and scoop up the puppy in his arms. "Gotcha!" he said.

The puppy squirmed and whimpered. "Aw, it's okay," said Mr. Santiago. "You're going to be fine. You're going to be more than fine—you're going to be the Petersons' next foster puppy."

Lizzie gulped. She wasn't so sure Mom would agree with that. But what choice did she have? As it was, Lizzie was late for her dog-walking clients. She was going to have to drop this puppy off at home until they could figure out what to do next. "Let's get her into the crate," she said. "And then maybe you could give us a ride home?"

CHAPTER FOUR

"You've got to be kidding!" Mom frowned at Lizzie and the puppy. "Lizzie, you know I'm on a deadline! Charles is at soccer practice, so he can't help. How am I supposed to take care of the Bean *and* a puppy?"

"It's only for, like, an hour," Lizzie promised. "Under an hour! I'll do my dog-walking route and come right back. The puppy can stay in the crate, and the Bean will sit and read to her."

The Bean liked to pretend to read to their foster puppies, just like his big brother, Charles, who enjoyed reading the Sunday comics to Buddy. Now, the Bean ran to grab a pile of his favorite picture books.

Mom sighed. "Fine," she said. "Go."

Lizzie grabbed her backpack and took off before Mom could change her mind. She raced to her first client's house and found Tank, a big German shepherd, waiting eagerly for his walk. "Sorry I'm late!" she told him as she snapped on his leash. She collected two other dogs along the way—three was the most she could handle at once—then dropped each one back at the right house when they'd had their walks. Then she started all over again with Samson, an old basset hound with long ears. Samson was a slow walker and a constant sniffer, and sometimes he took forever to get his "business" done. "Come on, come on," Lizzie said under her breath as she waited on the other end of the leash. Finally, he finished up and she marched him back to his house, double-time. Two more dogs, and she was finished. She raced back home, hoping to find the puppy dozing peacefully in the crate while the Bean turned pages and told the stories he knew by heart.

Instead, she found Mom, the Bean, Buddy, and the puppy all in the living room. Buddy and the puppy played tug with Buddy's favorite stuffie. The Bean sat on Mom's lap, listening to her read him one of the books he'd picked out. Mom looked up at Lizzie and shook her head. She did not look happy.

"Sorry, sorry, sorry!" Lizzie said. "I'll take them all out into the backyard. You go back to work."

Lizzie headed for the sliding door off the dining room, with both puppies and the Bean bounding along beside her.

"Finish!" The Bean waved his book at Lizzie. He hated it when people who were reading to him didn't get to the end of the story.

"We'll finish," said Lizzie as she slid the door open. "But let's just watch these puppies play for a while first." She needed to catch her breath.

Buddy and the new puppy zoomed out the door and scrambled down the stairs. Then they began to race around the yard, barking happily.

"Shhhh!" the Bean shouted. "Quiet! Mama's working!"

The puppies ignored him. Lizzie decided to distract them. "Hey, puppies, what's this?" She waved Buddy's favorite toy football, then threw it. They both tore after it. The new puppy pounced on it first and ran off with Buddy chasing her. Lizzie shook her head. "This girl sure is full of energy," she said. At least she couldn't bark with her mouth full, and Buddy didn't usually bark unless another dog started it.

"Come here, guys," Lizzie called after they'd run for a while. "I've got treats." She sat down on the grass and opened up a stick of string cheese from her pocket. Buddy came running. Cheese was his favorite, and he could smell it a mile away.

The new puppy came running, too. She sat a little way off and cocked her head.

What do you have there? Do I get some?

Lizzie called her over, patting her knee and holding out a small piece of cheese. The puppy approached slowly, then grabbed a piece from Lizzie's hand. She chewed and gulped, then looked back up into Lizzie's eyes. She wagged her tail and winked her sparkly eyes.

Yum. Got any more of that?

It only took a few more bites of cheese to get the puppy to lay down next to Lizzie, relaxed for the first time since Lizzie had met her. "Good dog," she said. "That's more like it." She picked up the Bean's book. "Now we can finish our story." First she pulled off her sweatshirt. The sun was warm even though the air was crisp.

The Bean leaned against Lizzie as she opened the book and began to read. "We'll start from the beginning, okay?" she asked. The Bean nodded sleepily.

When Lizzie finished the last page, she looked down to see the Bean fast asleep beside her. Next to him was Buddy, snoring softly. His front legs twitched, which meant he was probably dreaming about chasing a squirrel. Or—being chased by the new puppy? Lizzie looked down at her other side and burst out laughing. The new puppy was snuggled down inside Lizzie's sweatshirt as if it was a doggy sleeping bag. Her little white-and-brown face peeked out, eyes shut tight. She was even more adorable when she was asleep.

CHAPTER FIVE

Lizzie heard the sliding door open behind her, and a few moments later Mom joined her on the grass. She yawned and stretched out her arms. "I should write some more, but I'm tired," she said. "Plus, we have to figure out what we're going to do about this little gal." She nodded at the puppy, who was still sacked out.

"What do you mean, what are we going to do about her?" Lizzie asked. "Aren't we going to foster her?"

"Oh, Lizzie, it's really not a good time," Mom began.

"But, Mom," Lizzie pleaded, interrupting her.

"Caring Paws is full, and the puppy won't have anywhere else to go!" Caring Paws was the animal shelter where Lizzie volunteered. Recently they had taken in a whole bunch of dogs and cats who had just been through a big storm down south. The place was packed.

Mom folded her arms. "We won't be able to afford to foster puppies if I miss my deadline and lose my job," she said.

Lizzie folded her arms, too. "That would never happen," she said. "First of all, you never miss deadlines, and second of all, they would never fire you. They love you at that newspaper!"

Mom laughed. "I know, I'm being dramatic." Then she got serious. "But, Lizzie, this puppy is a real handful. How am I going to deal with her when you're at school?"

Lizzie pointed to the puppy, still snuggled into her sweatshirt. "I know she's kind of hyper," she said. "But she does settle down. Look at her, all cozied up in there. I think she likes being tucked in like that."

"Hmm." Mom raised her eyebrows. "Reminds me of how I used to swaddle you and your brothers when you were babies. When you were fussy, I'd wrap you up snug in your baby blanket, and you'd settle right down."

The puppy woke up just then, rolling over and yawning a pink-tongued puppy yawn. She let out the cutest little squeaks and snuffles as she pushed her way out of the sweatshirt and shook herself off.

Well, that sure was a refreshing nap! Now what are we going to do?

"Well, if we're going to keep her, I guess we'll have to take her to Dr. Gibson to see if she's micro-chipped," Mom said. By now, the Petersons knew all the steps to take when they found a stray dog. "And put up some signs and post online, asking if anyone's lost a dog."

Lizzie felt her heart rise. Now it was official: They had a new foster puppy. "What are we going to call her?" she asked. Naming the puppies they fostered was one of Lizzie's favorite things to do, even if the names only ended up being temporary. Every puppy had a special personality, and Lizzie loved trying to find the exact right fit.

Mom gazed down at the puppy, who had started to jump on Buddy to wake the older dog up. "She sure has a lot of energy," Mom said. "She's full of tricks."

"That's it!" said Lizzie. "Trixie!"

Just then, the puppy flicked her gaze toward Lizzie and cocked her head.

I like it! Say it again.

"Trixie." Mom nodded. "That works. Plus, it's kind of a Halloween-y name, as in trick or treat." She looked at Lizzie. "That reminds me, have you—"

Lizzie groaned and shook her head. She knew what Mom was going to ask. Halloween was only a few days away, and Lizzie still hadn't figured out her costume. Wasn't Halloween supposed to be a fun holiday? It used to be when Lizzie was little. This year, it just felt stressful. Everybody was talking about their costumes, and every costume she'd heard about was so clever, and creative, and cool. It wasn't enough anymore to plop on a tall black hat and say you were a witch.

Charles knew what he was going to be: an astronaut. Dad was helping him make a suit out of cardboard, painted white. And Mom had the Bean's costume ready to go: He was going to be an avocado. Lizzie didn't really get it, but she had to admit he looked adorable in his pudgy green outfit.

"Nope," Lizzie said. "Haven't decided." It was hard to come up with a costume when she wasn't into princesses or fairies or angels. Or robots or superheroes. Or scary things like mummies. What was left?

"You'll figure it out," Mom said. She had learned not to offer ideas after Lizzie had said no to everything she'd suggested so far: a ghost, a flower child, and a scientist. No, no, no.

Just then, the puppy's ears twitched. Her nose went up. Her eyes sparkled. She let out one short, loud bark, then dashed around the yard. Buddy couldn't resist dashing after her. The puppy ran even faster, peering back over her shoulder at Buddy.

Yes! That's it! Chase me!

Out by the swing set, Trixie stopped suddenly and whirled around. Buddy knew exactly what to do: He whirled around, too, and took off at a mad gallop with Trixie at his heels. Trixie's ears flapped in the wind, and her eyes were bright as both wild puppies zipped by Lizzie, Mom, and the Bean.

This is so much fun! Now I'm chasing you!

"Trixie!" shouted the Bean, clapping his hands as the puppies rushed past.

The puppy screeched to a halt again, but this time, she didn't whirl around to let Buddy chase her. This time, she trotted right over to the Bean and lay down, panting happily, in front of him.

Whatever you want to call me is fine with me! We're friends now.

Lizzie and her mom exchanged an *awww, so cute!* look. "Trixie it is," said Mom. She got up and brushed off her pants. "Keep these puppies playing, Lizzie. Trixie needs to burn off all the extra energy she can."

CHAPTER SIX

Lizzie had a hard time staying focused in school the next day. She just wanted to be with Trixie and watch her race around with all that happy energy. "I wonder what Trixie's life was like before we found her," Lizzie said to Maria as they worked on their dioramas for book reports. Lizzie was doing a wilderness scene for her favorite book, *Mountain Girl*. She had already made a Mountain Girl paper doll with long braids, a backpack, and hiking boots. Maria was working on an ocean scene for a book she'd read about sharks.

Lizzie always wondered about the previous lives of her family's foster puppies, especially the strays. Some stray dogs looked as if they'd been living on their own for some time. They needed baths, lots of extra food, and sometimes even medical care from the Petersons' vet, Dr. Gibson. Others, like Trixie, looked like they'd had pretty easy lives. Had Trixie run away from home and gotten lost? Did her people abandon her? Lizzie knew she might never find out. They'd had the puppy checked right away for a microchip, and there wasn't one. And nobody had responded to their "Found Dog" notices and posts. For now, Trixie's other life was a mystery.

Lizzie glued down some blue paper to represent the lake where Mountain Girl liked to fish and swim. "I just hope Trixie didn't drive Mom crazy today," she told Maria. "She is a little, um . . ." Lizzie was already in love with Trixie and she didn't want to say anything bad about her.

"Extra-extra?" Maria suggested.

Lizzie grinned. "That's Trixie," she said. "Extra wild, extra happy—and extra sweet and snuggly once you get her settled down."

After school, Lizzie raced home. What would she find when she got there? She was prepared to take Trixie and the Bean with her on her dog-walking route. The Bean was home from day care again, and Lizzie knew Mom would be more than ready for a break.

"Hello?" she called when she got home.

"Up here!" Mom called from upstairs.

Lizzie headed up, hoping to find Mom hard at work in her office. She was in the office—but she wasn't working. She was laughing so hard that tears streamed down her face. She wiped her eyes and grinned at Lizzie. "We've had a fun day," she said.

"I can see that," said Lizzie. The room was strewn with bright blobs of clothing, costumes, and accessories. "You got into the dress-up trunk." She started to laugh, too. There, sprawled amidst the mess, was Trixie, wearing a yellow dress that had belonged to one of Lizzie's dolls. She had a purple scarf draped around her neck, and on her head was a golden (cardboard) crown with beautiful (painted) jewels. "Queen Trixie!" Lizzie said. Trixie looked totally regal and totally goofy, all at the same time. She waggled her head and the crown slipped sideways.

Next to her was the Bean, dressed in a wizard's cape and hat, red cowboy boots, and a pink tutu that Lizzie had worn nonstop when she was three. The Bean waved a silver wand at Lizzie. "Ta-da!" he said.

Buddy, meanwhile, lay on his bed under Mom's desk, ignoring the whole thing. He had never enjoyed getting dressed up. Lizzie spotted a few of the costumes they had tried to get him to wear:

a wiener dog outfit, a flowerpot, and a mail delivery person. Buddy had refused to wear any of them for more than a minute. He would squirm out of costumes, chew up wigs, and try to hide under the furniture.

"You wouldn't believe how much fun we've had today," said Mom. "No matter what we put on Trixie, she likes it. Playing dress-up really keeps her calm—and it keeps the Bean happy, too."

The Bean twirled in his cape. "Super-Bean!" he yelled.

"Does Super-Bean want to come walk dogs with me?" Lizzie asked him. "And Super-Trixie, too, of course."

"Super-Bean says 'yes!'" the Bean said, jumping up and down.

Trixie jumped up and down, too. The crown fell off. Her ears stood straight up and her eyes twinkled.

"Great, Lizzie," said Mom. "All I need is an hour or two of quiet and I can get a lot done." She looked around at the piles of costumes and clothing and sighed. "Once I get this mess cleaned up, that is."

"I'll help." Lizzie bent down to pick up a fuzzy brown item. "Aww." She held up a small, tattered fleece hoodie. "The Bean's 'fur.' Remember when he loved to pretend that he was a dog?"

"Ruff, ruff!" said the Bean.

Mom and Lizzie laughed as they stuffed things back into the trunk. Lizzie found a pair of brown antlers attached to a headband. "Buddy couldn't stand to wear these," she said. "But I bet I know someone who would love them."

"And this," Mom pulled out a bright-orange puffy coat, with green leaves hanging off it. "Remember? The pumpkin costume?"

45

Lizzie cracked up, remembering how hard they'd tried to get a family photo with Buddy wearing the pumpkin costume. "Don't even let Buddy see that," she said. "He'll get all grumpy and try to tear it to bits." She held up a dog shirt made to look like a tuxedo, and the top hat that went with it. "We tried everything with him, didn't we?"

"We sure did. And now all these costumes are just sitting in the trunk," Mom said. "That's kind of a shame. They're all so adorable. Who can resist a puppy in costume?"

Lizzie looked down at the tuxedo costume, then up at her mom. She felt that tingly feeling that meant she was about to have a good idea.

Lizzie dropped the tuxedo sweater. "I'll finish cleaning up later. I have to call Ms. Dobbins," she said.

Lizzie had a lot of good ideas. But now and then

a really *great* one came along, and when it did she didn't like to waste any time. Why wait? She liked to move right on to making the great idea into a reality.

Plus, there really wasn't any time to waste on this idea. She ran right downstairs and grabbed the phone to dial the number for Caring Paws, the animal shelter where Ms. Dobbins was the director.

"I know that Halloween is right around the corner," she said all in a rush. Ms. Dobbins had barely had a chance to say hello. "But I know just how to help out with your overcrowding problem."

CHAPTER SEVEN

"Oooh, Trixie! You're looking fabulous and fancy, like a princess!" Maria cooed, later that day. She and Lizzie met at their usual corner after they'd finished up their dog-walking routes. After she had talked with Ms. Dobbins, Lizzie had begged her mom to text Maria just to let her know something was up. Then she'd headed off with Trixie and the Bean.

"I know, right?" Lizzie asked. "Trixie looks great in yellow."

"And I love your outfit, too," Maria told the Bean. "Very creative."

The Bean spun around happily, waving a wand

and stomping his cowboy boots on the sidewalk.

Trixie took the cue and began to spin around herself. Her crown was even more crooked now, and her dress dragged on the ground, but she was obviously very pleased with herself.

Check it out! Who's the fairest of them all?

Maria and Lizzie laughed.

Maria linked her arm in Lizzie's as they began to walk along. "So come on, I know you're dying to tell me! What's the great idea?"

"Okay, so you know how Trixie likes to dress up, right?" Lizzie asked.

"Uh, yeah." Maria pointed at the pint-sized pup.

"But do you remember how much Buddy hated it?" Lizzie went on. "And do you remember how we tried all kinds of different costumes on him?"

Maria cracked up. "Oh, how could I ever forget

him squirming out of that pumpkin outfit?"

"He couldn't get out fast enough," said Lizzie. "Anyway, so we have a whole pile of costumes to give away. And Ms. Dobbins has a shelter full of dogs that need to be adopted. And so"—Lizzie held out a hand—"wait for it—I came up with the idea of a costume contest!"

"Because nobody can resist—" Maria began.

"A dog in costume!" they finished together.

Maria gave Lizzie a high five. "It really is a great idea," she said. "But wait. Halloween is only a few days away. How could Ms. Dobbins ever pull something like that together so fast?"

"Because she won't be on her own," Lizzie said. "I promised we'd help. Daphne and Brianna, too."

"Lizzie!" Maria said. "Without even asking us first?"

"I knew you wouldn't want to miss out." Lizzie grinned at her friend.

Maria rolled her eyes and shook her head, but she was smiling.

"Let's start planning," Lizzie said, pulling her friend along on the sidewalk. "My mom already checked with your mom, and you're eating dinner at my house."

Back at Lizzie's, the girls found Mom in the kitchen, starting dinner. "Thanks so much for taking the Bean and Trixie," Mom said. She handed Lizzie and Maria a few carrot sticks to snack on. "I got a lot of writing done in a short amount of time once it was quiet around here."

"We'll go upstairs and finish cleaning up all the costumes," Lizzie said. "Then we're going to work on signs. And make a list of where to post them, and figure out what our prizes should be, and line up judges, and—"

"And have a good dinner, and get to bed early so you'll have lots of energy for everything else you have to do." Mom shooed them away. "I'll call you when we're ready to eat."

Trixie, the Bean, and Buddy followed Lizzie and Maria upstairs. When they walked into Mom's study where all the costumes were, Buddy turned right around and hurried back downstairs.

Maria laughed. "I don't think he's changed his mind about dressing up," she said as they watched him go.

Trixie and the Bean, on the other hand, waded right in and started to check out the costumes. Trixie grabbed a squirrel costume in her teeth and shook it happily while the Bean threw off his wizard's cloak and tutu, pulled on a pair of overalls, and replaced his wizard's hat with a fireman's hat.

Lizzie and Maria worked quickly to pick up the last costumes, fold them up, and then sort everything into piles: small, medium, and large. "This'll

make it easier for Ms. Dobbins and her staff to figure out which costume will work for which dog,"
Lizzie said. She folded a furry Wookie suit care-
fully before adding it to the "large" pile. Then
she turned to see Maria trying on an Alice in
Wonderland outfit, a blue dress with a white apron.

The dress was way too small, and Lizzie giggled. "I wore that when I was in second grade,"
she said. "I carried my favorite terrier stuffie in
a picnic basket and told everybody he was Toto."

"I bet you looked adorable," said Maria. "My
best costume was also in second grade. I was a
computer. My dad helped me make it. I had blink-
ing lights and everything." Maria was also having
trouble figuring out what to be this Halloween.
"Too bad it's also too small for me now."

Lizzie put one last costume, fairy wings, on
the "medium" pile. "I think that's it. Hey, where's
Trixie?"

At the sound of her name, Trixie sat up. She had snuggled herself into the wizard cloak that the Bean had taken off. Now she wiggled happily and let out a yip.

Here I am!

"I have a feeling Trixie is excited about the costume contest," said Maria. "Whatever she wears, I'm sure someone will fall in love with her and want to take her home."

Lizzie felt a pang. Of course, finding new homes for puppies was what fostering was all about. But it was never easy to see them go. Trixie was really something special, and Lizzie wasn't quite ready to say good-bye.

CHAPTER EIGHT

"Can you believe this crowd?" Lizzie asked Maria. It was Saturday afternoon, the day before Halloween, and the costume contest in the parking lot of Caring Paws was in full swing. It was happy chaos as shelter employees and volunteers paraded the shelter dogs around. Each one looked better—or funnier, or cuter—than the last. Lizzie could hardly believe that her idea had come to life so perfectly.

"We are definitely going to get some of these cuties adopted today," Maria said.

"I agree," said someone from behind them.

Lizzie turned to see Ms. Dobbins in vampire fangs and a black cape. "I can't thank you girls enough for all you did to pull this together," she said. "I think this contest is going to have to become an annual event. And it's not just the dogs that need adoption who are here. Lots of people came with their own dogs—some of them rescues they got from this shelter—and they're having a fantastic time."

"I even talked to one couple who came without a dog," said Maria. "They just like to dress up. They had fantastic costumes. Like a really cool alien look for the guy and a space princess for the woman."

"Maybe we need to add a prize category for humans next year," said Lizzie. "Bonus points if you dress as a dog."

There was a scratchy sound as someone touched the microphone Ms. Dobbins had set up in the middle of a raised platform. "Testing, testing," said a familiar voice.

It was Lizzie's dad. He and the fire chief had been invited to be judges, along with Jerry Small, the owner of Lizzie's favorite bookstore, and Ms. Somers, who ran the hardware store. Dr. Gibson, the Petersons' vet, was the fifth judge.

Up onstage, Dad tapped the mic again. "Can you all hear me?" he asked. He wore an embarrassing beanie hat striped in red and yellow with a red propeller on top, baggy shorts, and an oversized "I ♥ Dogs" T-shirt. He looked like a gigantic, nerdy, eight-year-old boy.

Lizzie could hardly look at him, but Maria thought the costume was great. "Loud and clear!" Maria yelled to Mr. Peterson.

"And what are you girls dressed as?" Ms. Dobbins asked while looking them up and down. "I think I can guess. Dog walkers, right?"

"Exactly!" Lizzie said. She spun around, showing Ms. Dobbins the back of her sweatshirt. She, Maria, Daphne, and Brianna were all wearing them. They had arrived in the mail that morning, a fantastic surprise from Mom. The sweatshirt was exactly like Lizzie's old one, except for its color—dark green. Also, it had writing on the back: "Need a dog walker? Call AAA Dynamic Dog Walkers!" The shirts had immediately become the official uniform for AAA—and solved Lizzie's costume problem. "I bet we'll pick up some business here today."

The mic crackled again. "Okay, people, it's time for the parade!" Dad said. "Chief Olson will show you where to line up, and then you'll pass by the judge's stand."

Doctor Gibson, who wore kitty ears and had whiskers painted on her cheeks, leaned into the mic. "We've got all kinds of great prizes, like a free checkup at my veterinarian office, and gift certificates for books and hardware. And there are lots of categories. Cutest, best-dressed, funniest, most look-alike with owner. So, get ready to show off those fabulous costumes!"

There was a flurry of movement as people and dogs organized themselves into a line. Lizzie grinned down at Trixie as she and Maria joined the parade. "You are rocking that pumpkin costume," Lizzie told the little pup. Trixie's adorable face stuck out above the puffy orange outfit, her little twinkle-toe feet stuck out below, and her tail wagged at the other end. She wore an orange-and-green hat that looked like the top and stem of the pumpkin.

Trixie cocked her head and sat up, holding her paws in front of her.

I know, I know!

"She should win cutest," said Maria.

"That's what I think, too," said Lizzie. "But there's a lot of competition. I mean, look around!" They were surrounded by dogs in all kinds of costumes. Lizzie spotted a couple of Buddy's old ones: the Wookie and the tuxedo. She also saw a cowboy outfit, a ballerina, and a very cool dragon. People had really gotten into dressing up their dogs.

"Well, you really don't want to give Trixie up quite yet, anyway, do you?" Maria asked.

Lizzie smiled at her friend as the parade began to move ahead. "You really do know me," she said. Then she waved at Dad as they paraded past the judge's stand. He had promised not to play favorites, but Lizzie saw his eyes light up when he spotted Trixie. He and the whole family had fallen in love with the happy little pup.

Then they were beyond the judges and walking back the way they had come, doubling past the rest of the parade. "Oh, those must be the people you mentioned," Lizzie said to Maria. She nodded at a couple in costume. "I love how she's a princess, but she's not wearing a big frilly gown," She admired the woman's stretchy neon pink jumpsuit. "I mean, she's a space princess, right?" The costumes really looked professional.

"With an alien boyfriend," Maria said, giggling. "I love his ears." His ears were silver and about a foot long—and there were three of them.

Lizzie saw the couple looking back at them, so she waved and smiled. They waved back— but not at Lizzie. They were waving at Trixie. Lizzie noticed that Trixie was getting a lot of attention: Everybody cooed over how cute she was in her costume. But was she the cutest dog there? Lizzie was counting on Trixie winning that category.

There was another tapping on the mic. "What a

great parade! You all look so fantastic," said Jerry Smalls. "We wish we could give every one of you a prize. We judges are going to confer for a few minutes, and then we'll come back and announce the winners."

Lizzie felt her heart thumping fast. If Trixie won the "cutest" prize, she'd get to parade across the stage. Everyone would see her—and Lizzie was sure that someone in that crowd would want to take her home.

CHAPTER NINE

Lizzie and Maria stood on line at the apple cider stand while they waited for the big announcement.

"I love our new dog-walking uniform," Maria said, looking down at her sweatshirt.

"Me too," said Lizzie. "I've decided to wear this when we trick-or-treat tomorrow, too. Why not?"

"I will, too, then." Maria threw an arm around Lizzie's shoulder. "Problem solved—and it's good advertising."

Just as they paid for their cider, Lizzie heard the mic crackle again. "It's time!" she said. She grabbed Maria's sleeve, and they took off back toward the stage with Trixie trotting along. Lizzie held up crossed fingers. "Come on, come on," she whispered. Trixie just *had* to win cutest.

Jerry Smalls spoke into the mic. "Well, you made our job hard today," he said. "And we want to offer congratulations to everyone who came. But we do have a few winners to announce. The first prize we'll hand out is for funniest costume. This dog is a visitor here at Caring Paws. She lost her home in a hurricane and she's hoping to find a new one today! Skye gets a blue ribbon and whoever decides to adopt her will receive a gift card to my bookshop." He held up both.

One of the shelter volunteers gave a happy shriek and led a cute poodle mix up to the stage to collect her ribbon. The crowd laughed and clapped.

"That is a pretty funny costume," Lizzie said to Maria. "I mean—a giant pickle?" They laughed and applauded along with everyone else.

Now Dr. Gibson took the mic. "Next, we have a prize for the most creative costume. Come on up, Max—or should I say Elvis? Max was adopted from Caring Paws last May, and I hear he's very happy with his new family."

Everybody clapped for the small brown pug, who wore a white rhinestone cape, sunglasses, and a black wig. The young boy who'd led him onstage bent down to give him a big hug.

Lizzie and Maria clapped some more as Dr. Gibson gave the boy a blue ribbon and a gallon of apple cider.

Chief Olson got up to announce the next prize, for the scariest costume. "We're awarding this one to Nora, in her skeleton costume," he said. Nora, a huge gray Great Dane, charged toward the stage as soon as she heard her name, towing her owner behind her. The big dog wore a black hoodie with white bone design. The hood even pulled up to look like a skull. "Whoa, Nora!" said the chief as the big dog lunged for the ribbon.

"Sorry, sorry," said her owner, a small young woman. She grabbed Nora's leash.

"That's okay, she just couldn't wait to get her prize," said the chief. "I think she'll really enjoy it, too." He held out a giant bone-shaped biscuit. "What do you think, Nora? Kind of matches your outfit."

Nora accepted the biscuit and pranced off the stage with her head and tail high, showing off her prize.

Then Dad came to the mic. "I know everybody's waiting on this one," he said, "so here goes. It was really, really hard to pick a winner for the cutest costume category. I mean, we all have cuteness overload today, right?"

The crowd applauded, but Lizzie was too busy crossing her fingers. "Come on, Trixie, come on!"

she said under her breath. Trixie sat at attention, her head cocked and both ears perked up.

Sure! Where are we going?

Lizzie ruffled the happy little pup's ears. Trixie had never looked more adorable. Lizzie just knew that she was going to win. Why was her father taking so long to make this announcement?

Dad stepped away to check on something with the other judges. Then he came back to the mic. "We actually have a tie in this category, so the winners will each get a ribbon and a prize. Our first winner is Hercules, another new visitor here at Caring Paws."

A volunteer whooped and ran toward the stage, leading a tall hound mix with big floppy ears. The dog was dressed in a pirate outfit, complete with a parrot stuffie riding on his back. Lizzie had to admit that he was totally adorable. She clapped, waiting for Dad to announce the other winner, which obviously had to be Trixie.

Dad handed over a ribbon. "The prize in this category happens to be a free checkup with Dr. Gibson. That will be perfect for whoever adopts Hercules. Arrr, me hearties!"

Lizzie rolled her eyes. If there was anything more embarrassing than your dad dressing up like a little kid, it was your dad doing a bad pirate voice.

"And, now, our other winner in the cutest category," Dad went on, thankfully in his normal voice.

Lizzie held her breath and gripped Maria's hand.

"Lena, the beautiful flower," Dad finished.

Lizzie shook her head. She must have heard wrong. Wasn't he supposed to say Trixie?

Dad waved at a couple in the crowd. "We loved how Lena and her owners coordinated their costumes," Dad said as the couple trotted toward the stage. The couple were dressed in hippie outfits: patched jeans, fringed suede vests, sandals, and love beads. Their dog, a Pomeranian, was dressed as a pretty pink flower. The young woman, who had long, flowing hair, held the tiny dog in her arms.

"Flower Power!" Dad said, raising a fist.

Lizzie shook her head again. Wasn't it bad enough that Trixie hadn't won? Why did he have to keep embarrassing her?

Maria gave Lizzie's hand a squeeze. "It's okay," she said. "We know who the real winner is." She smiled down at Trixie.

But Lizzie couldn't smile. Not yet. She had really, really wanted Trixie to win. Now the contest was over.

But—it wasn't.

Ms. Dobbins took the mic again. "And finally," she said. "We have one more prize to give out. This is the grand prize, for best costume overall."

Lizzie sighed with relief. This explained why Trixie hadn't won the cutest category. She had a much bigger prize coming to her!

CHAPTER TEN

"Okay, this is it," Lizzie said to Trixie. "You are going to look fabulous on that fire truck."

Trixie looked up at her, wagged her whole little butt, and let out a happy yip.

Whatever it is, I can't wait! You make it sound so exciting.

"Um, Lizzie," said Maria.

Lizzie knew exactly what Maria was thinking. Best friends were like that. She held up a hand. "I know, you're going to say that they haven't announced the winner yet, and that you're worried I might be disappointed. Well, sometimes you're right about things, but sometimes I am. I just *know* that Trixie is going to—"

"And the winner is," Ms. Dobbins said a little too loudly. The mic squealed, and Lizzie couldn't quite hear what she'd said. It didn't matter. Of course it was Trixie! Lizzie could see her dad up there, and he looked really happy. She started to walk toward the stage, holding Trixie's leash proudly.

Ms. Dobbins waited until the mic had quieted down. "Sorry! To repeat: The winner is another of our wonderful guests here at Caring Paws. Come on up, Boots!"

Lizzie stopped in her tracks. Her shoulders sagged. Boots? What?

Then she saw a shelter volunteer leading a bull-dog she'd seen in the parade. He was adorable, and he had the kind of face anyone could love: all wrinkly, with big brown eyes and droopy ears. He looked fantastic in the tuxedo outfit Lizzie and her mom had donated. "He is pretty cute," said Maria.

"Sure," said Lizzie. "But is 'pretty cute' really better than Trixie?" Lizzie frowned at her father up on the stage. What was he—what were all the judges—thinking?

She felt a hand on her shoulder. "What a fun day, Lizzie," her mom said. She'd arrived late but in time for the final prize. "You girls did a great job organizing this."

"But Trixie didn't win," Lizzie said. She knew she was pouting, but she couldn't help it. "I mean, didn't Dad even vote for her?"

"Ask him," said Mom. Lizzie turned to see Dad walking toward her.

Lizzie crossed her arms and glared at him. "Dad," she said.

"I know, Lizzie. You thought Trixie should've won. I thought so, too, at first. But then I thought about how good you are at finding excellent homes for our foster puppies. Boots needed more help. He's a bigger, older dog, and Ms. Dobbins is sure that a new owner will see him here or at tomorrow's parade downtown."

"That makes sense," Maria said. "Look, he's already getting a ton of attention." There was a cluster of people around Boots.

Lizzie knew her father was right. She knew she wouldn't have a hard time finding a good home for a dog as special as Trixie—whether or not the puppy had won the Grand Prize. But she was still disappointed.

"Let's just go home," she said. She didn't feel like staying for the refreshments they'd organized.

"Oh, come on, Lizzie. You know you want one of those chocolate pupcakes my dad made," Maria said. She pointed at the puppy pulling on Lizzie's leash. "And I think Trixie wants to congratulate the winner."

Lizzie let Trixie and Maria pull her toward the stage, where all the winners and other paraders milled about. The people already had cupcakes in their hands, and the dogs were happily crunching the homemade biscuits Lizzie and Maria had made.

"Congratulations," Maria said to the volunteer who was walking Boots.

"He totally deserves it," she said. "He is the sweetest boy! I just know this will help him find a great home." She smiled down at Trixie, who was pawing playfully at Boots. "Your dog is really cute, too."

"She's a foster," Lizzie said. "We're trying to find her a home."

"Well, definitely bring her to the parade

tomorrow," said the woman. "She'll get a lot of exposure there, even if she's not riding in the fire truck. Boots is going to be soooo excited about that!"

Lizzie was just about to tell the woman that her family had donated Boots's costume when she felt someone tap her on the shoulder. She turned to see the woman in the shiny pink space princess costume.

"Did I just hear you say that this dog is a foster?" The woman pointed at Trixie.

Lizzie nodded. "Yup, we're looking for a home for her."

"Really?" The woman's eyes grew wide. "Wait until my husband hears that." She turned to wave at the alien who'd been with her earlier. "Ned!"

Lizzie almost giggled. Ned was kind of a funny name for an alien. But then she heard what the woman said next. "She's available!" she called. "She's looking for a home!"

Ned-the-alien started to work his way through the crowd toward them. "You're kidding," he said when he got there and saw his wife on her knees, petting Trixie. "That's the best news I've heard in a long time."

"We are crazy about this dog!" the woman said. She was letting Trixie plant kisses all over her face. "We've been watching her all day. She looks so at home in that costume—does she like to dress up?"

Lizzie and Maria broke out laughing. "She loves it! It's, like, her favorite thing to do," said Lizzie.

"Same with us," said Ned. "Vicky and I travel to events all over the country where we can dress up in different costumes and hang out with other people who are into cosplay."

"And this pup is just the right size to be totally portable. She could go everywhere with us." Now Vicky had Trixie in her arms, snuggling her.

The man cleared his throat and looked at Mom and Dad, who had just joined them. "Um, just so you know, we do have jobs and a house and stuff," he said. "We work from home, for ourselves. We design video games. And we've had dogs before. We know how to take care of them. We came here today hoping to find the right dog to adopt—and I think we have."

"Huh," said Dad. "What do you think, Lizzie?"

Lizzie thought it was fantastic—and awful. She could already tell that Trixie had met her perfect forever family. That was the fantastic part. And the awful part? Well, she was sort of used to that since she'd done it so many times. Saying good-bye to another foster pup was always bittersweet.

"Well, I think Trixie just won the best prize of all today," Lizzie said. She felt tears coming, but she blinked them back and smiled at Ned and Vicky. "She's going to have a really fun life with you. Just promise me one thing: promise to send us lots of pictures of Trixie in all her costumes!"

PUPPY TIPS

Does your dog like to dress up? Some dogs seem to enjoy it. It is true that wearing clothes can help calm some dogs down; there are special close-fitting shirts that can make dogs feel more secure during thunderstorms, for example. And some dogs love the attention they get when they're out in public wearing a cute outfit.

You can give it a try with a simple jacket or a bandanna collar. Don't force it, though; if your dog seems unhappy when you experiment with dress-up, it's best to let the idea go.

Dear Reader,

My dog, Zipper, gets very excited when I get out the neon orange vest he wears when we walk in the woods. The vest makes him easier for me to spot and helps keep him safe during hunting season here in Vermont. He also has a warm red coat that he wears in winter, since his fur is very short and he gets cold easily. But I don't think Zipper would enjoy wearing a pirate outfit!

Yours from the Puppy Place,

Ellen Miles

THE PUPPY PLACE

Want to read about another fun, active puppy? Try SWEETIE or PUGSLEY.

ABOUT THE AUTHOR

Ellen Miles loves dogs, which is why she has a great time writing the Puppy Place books. And guess what? She loves cats, too! (In fact, her very first pet was a beautiful tortoiseshell cat named Jenny.) That's why she came up with the Kitty Corner series. Ellen lives in Vermont and loves to be outdoors with her dog, Zipper, every day, walking, biking, skiing, or swimming, depending on the season. She also loves to read, cook, explore her beautiful state, play with dogs, and hang out with friends and family.

Visit Ellen at ellenmiles.net.